Franklin and the Radio

Kids Can Press

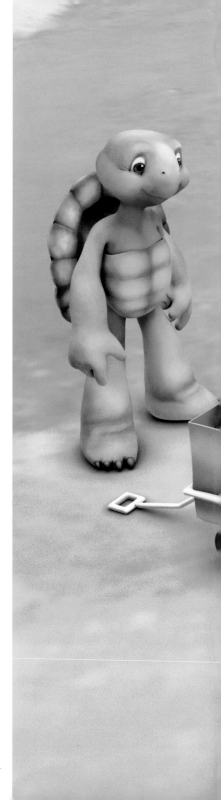

Every year, Franklin and his family had a Turtle Family Clean-Up and Giveaway Day. They sorted through all their old stuff.

"Where are you going to put your blocks, Harriet?" Franklin asked. "In the giveaway box or the junk box?"

"Giveaway," said Harriet. "They're still good."

"How about your radio, Franklin?" Mr. Turtle asked.

"Well, it *was* a birthday present," said Franklin, "but it's old and broken now, so I think it goes in the junk box."

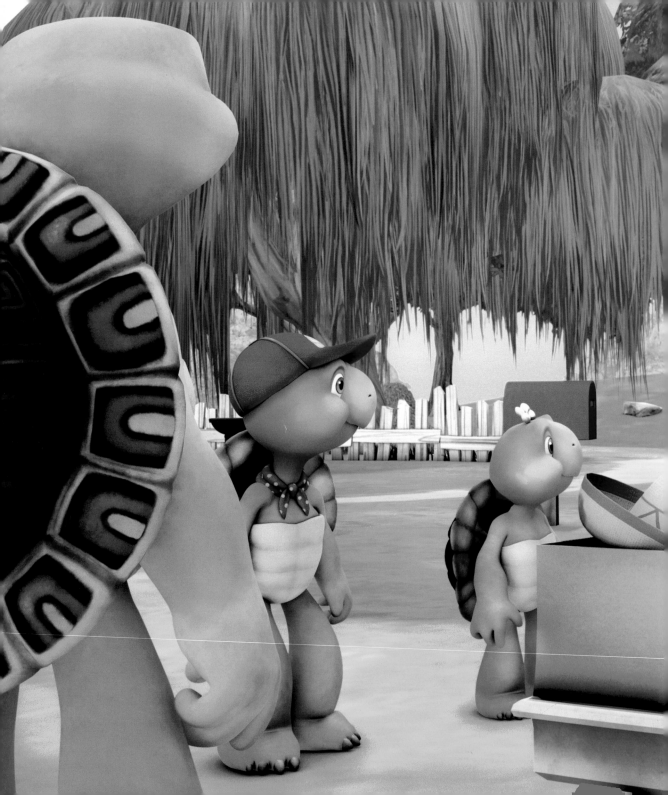

"Hi, guys!" Aunt T said, walking up to the house. "What are you up to?"

"It's Turtle Family Clean-Up and Giveaway Day," said Franklin. "See? We have a junk box and a giveaway box."

"Neat!" said Aunt T. She looked through the giveaway box and pulled out a book. "I've always wanted to read this!"

"You can have it," said Mr. Turtle.

"Really?" said Aunt T. "Thanks!"

"My pleasure," said Mr. Turtle. Then he turned to Franklin. "Can you help me bring the junk to the Foxes' junkyard?"

"Okay, Dad," said Franklin.

Franklin and Mr. Turtle wheeled the junk box in their wagon over to the Foxes' junkyard.

"Hello?" Franklin called when they got there. "Anyone here?"

"Hi, Franklin!" said Fox, coming out of his house.

"Hi, Fox," said Franklin. "We brought some junk for the junkyard."

"Great!" said Fox. He peered into the box. "Hey, is this a radio?"
"Yeah, but it doesn't work anymore," said Franklin.
"Do you mind if I take it?" Fox asked. "My dad can fix anything!"
"Sure," said Franklin. "It's all yours!"
"Thanks!" said Fox.

The next day after school, Franklin's friends gathered in the playground.
"What's going on?" Franklin asked.
"You have to see this!" said Bear.
"Ta-da!" said Fox, holding up a radio. It was painted blue and red, and there were stars all over it.

"Wow!" said Franklin. "Is that the same radio I gave you?"

"Yep!" said Fox. "My dad helped me fix it, and then I decorated it
with some paint, stickers and ribbon."

"That's the best radio ever!" said Rabbit.

"Yeah!" everyone else agreed.

"It sure is …" Franklin said.

Fox turned on the radio, and everyone started dancing to the music. Franklin tried to have fun, but he couldn't take his eyes off the radio. When the song ended, Franklin waved to his friends. "I have to go," he said. "See you later." He headed off toward home.

"What's wrong, Franklin?" Bear asked, catching up to his friend.

"Well …" said Franklin, hesitating. "I guess I just wish I'd realized how cool-io that radio was before I gave it away."

"Yeah," said Bear, nodding.

Neither Bear nor Franklin realized that Fox had heard them talking.

"Wait, Franklin!" Fox called, grabbing the radio and running up to them. "I ... uh ... want you to have this. It was yours first. I'm sure my dad and I can make another one."

"Really?" said Franklin, perking up. "Wow! Thanks, Fox!"

"Sure," said Fox, handing Franklin the radio. "Okay. See you tomorrow." He took one last look at the radio and then started for home.

Franklin and Bear brought the radio back to where Beaver, Goose and Snail were practicing their dance moves.

"Hey, guys," Franklin said. "How about some more music?"

"Isn't that Fox's radio?" asked Beaver.

"He just gave it back to me," said Franklin.

"Why would he do that?" Beaver asked. "He loved that radio!"

Franklin shrugged. "I don't know," he said.

"Sorry, Franklin," said Goose. "Beaver, Snail and I have to work on our school project. Maybe we can play with the radio tomorrow."

"Okay," said Franklin, a little disappointed. "Bye, guys."

"Bye, Franklin!" they called as they headed off. "Bye, Bear!"

Franklin and Bear went to Franklin's house to play with the radio.

"This radio really is cool-io!" said Bear, dancing to the music. "Fox sure did a great job fixing it up!"

"Yeah!" said Franklin, bopping to the beat.

"His paint job is really nice!" said Bear.

"Definitely …" said Franklin, slowing down.

"And I love those star stickers!"

"Uh-huh," said Franklin, stopping. A worried look crossed his face.

"What's the matter?" Bear asked. "Aren't you happy to have the radio back?"

"I don't know," said Franklin. "Something just doesn't feel right."

The next morning, Franklin brought the radio to school. He and his friends were dancing to the music when they heard a loud *SCREECH!*

"What was that?" Beaver asked.

"Sorry, guys!" said Fox, walking up to them. He held up an old radio. "It's my radio. I haven't totally fixed it yet." He turned it on again, and it let out another screech.

Everyone covered their ears.

"Don't worry, Fox," said Rabbit. "I'm sure you'll get it right, just like the other radio."

"Sure," said Fox, sighing. "I'm going to work on it after school."

"Good luck!" said Franklin.

"Take good care of that radio, Franklin," said Fox. "It's pretty special."

"I know," said Franklin.

After school, Mr. Turtle fixed Franklin a snack.

"Oh," he said, noticing the radio on the table. "Isn't that the radio you gave Fox? He sure put a lot of work into it!"

"Yeah," said Franklin.

"What's it doing here?" Mr. Turtle asked.

"Well, uh, he —" Franklin started saying.

Just then, Aunt T came in through the back door.

"This is the best book ever!" she said, holding up the book Mr. Turtle had given her. "You have to take it back!"

"No, no, no," said Mr. Turtle. "You keep it! I was going to give it away anyway, and seeing you enjoying it makes me happy."

"Hmmm," said Franklin, looking at the radio.

The next day, Franklin and his friends went to the Foxes' junkyard.
"Hi, guys!" Fox said, rooting through a barrel of parts.
"Hi, Fox," said Franklin. "Are you still trying to fix that radio?"
"Yep," said Fox. "I just can't seem to find the right pieces."

"Fox," said Franklin, "I've been thinking. I want you to have this one back." He held up Fox's old radio.

"But you love that radio!" said Fox. "And it was yours first."

"Yeah, but I gave it to you," said Franklin. "I shouldn't have taken it back." He smiled. "And it was way more fun seeing you happy with it, anyway."

"Thanks, Franklin," said Fox, smiling. "This radio really does make me happy." He paused. "But you know what would make me even happier? If you would help me get a dance party started!"

"You got it!" said Franklin, turning on the radio. "Who wants to try my new dance move?!"